THE COMPLETED
Hickory Dickory Dock

To L. Leslie Brooke, Randolph Caldecott, Kate Greenaway, Arthur Rackham,
Jessie Willcox Smith, Blanche Fisher Wright, et al., with love!
—*J. A.*

And to Mother Goose
—*E. C.*

THE COMPLETED
Hickory Dickory Dock

By Jim Aylesworth Illustrated by Eileen Christelow

New York 1990 Atheneum

Hickory, dickory, dock.
The mouse ran up the clock.

The clock struck one,
And down he run.
Hickory, dickory, dock.

Nibble on, bibble on, bees.
The mouse bit off some cheese.
The clock struck two,
Away he flew.
Nibble on, bibble on, bees.

Honeybee, bunny bee, boo.
The mouse ran into a shoe.
The clock struck three,
He scratched a flea.
Honeybee, bunny bee, boo.

Apple eye, dapple eye, day.
The mouse just loves to play.
The clock struck four,
He rolled on the floor.
Apple eye, dapple eye, day.

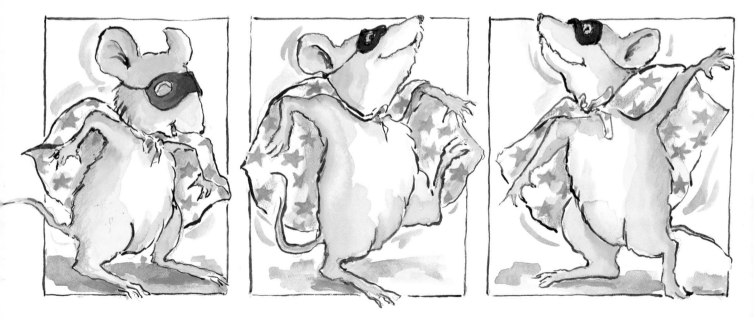

Milky Way, silky way, sat.
The mouse got chased by a cat.

The clock struck five,
He's glad he's alive.
Milky Way, silky way, sat.

Slippery, whippery, whirl.
The mouse showed off to a girl.
The clock struck six,
He finished his tricks.
Slippery, whippery, whirl.

Chickadee, rickadee, run.
His papa calls him Son.
The clock struck seven,
His real name is Kevin.
Chickadee, rickadee, run.

Icicle, bicycle, bert.
The mouse had pie for dessert.
The clock struck eight,
He licked the plate.
Icicle, bicycle, bert.

Splashery, dashery, dears.
The mouse washed off his ears.
The clock struck nine,
He gave them a shine.
Splashery, dashery, dears.

Peekaboo, teekaboo, took.
His mama read him a book.
The clock struck ten,
She read it again.
Peekaboo, teekaboo, took.

Tippytoe, hippytoe, head.
The mouse knelt by his bed.
The clock struck eleven,
His prayers went to heaven.
Tippytoe, hippytoe, head.

Silvery, bilvery, beams.
The mouse had wonderful dreams.
The clock struck twelve,
Now dream some yourselves.
Silvery, bilvery, beams.

First Aladdin Books edition 1994
Text copyright © 1990 by Jim Aylesworth
Illustrations copyright © 1990 by Eileen Christelow

Atheneum Books for Young Readers, Simon & Schuster Children's Publishing Division 1230 Avenue of the Americas,
New York, New York 10020. Printed in Belgium.

The Library of Congress has cataloged the hardcover edition as follows:
Aylesworth, Jim.   The completed hickory dickory dock/by Jim Aylesworth;
illustrated by Eileen Christelow.—1st ed.   p.   cm.   Summary: Completes the classic nursery rhyme about the mouse that ran up the clock.
1. Nursery rhymes.   2. Children's poetry.   [1. Nursery rhymes.]   I. Christelow, Eileen, ill.
II Title.   PZ8.3.A95Co   1990   398.8—dc20   89-38484   94-1226;   0-689-71862-4 (Aladdin pbk.)